Sonia —

You are wonderful.

Always BE YOU!

♡
Lissa

PIPSQUEAK
THE PUPPY

WRITTEN BY
LISSA WEBBER

ILLUSTRATED BY
TAMI BOYCE

ISBN-13: 978-0-692-18284-0

ARGONNE BOOKS LLC
Atlanta, Georgia

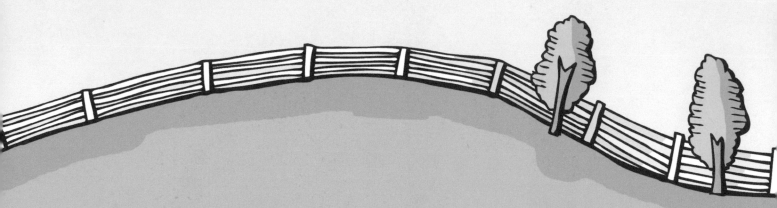

DEDiCATiON

For **CLAiRE**, who inspired me
to write this book;

for **RYAN**, whose grit taught me
to never give up;

for **JONATHAN**, who supports
everything I do;

and for **LADYBUG**, our
real-life Pipsqueak.

In spring Big Rover barked aloud and beamed with joyful pride,
"Our Mama Ruff has eight new perfect puppies by her side!"
The puppies frolicked in the fields, they tumbled all day long,
and watching them made all upon the farm break into song!

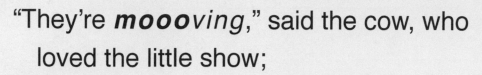

"They're **moooving**," said the cow, who
loved the little show;
"They're **baaa**rking," said the sheep,
her eyes were all aglow.
"What precious little **neigh**-bors," called
the biggest horse…
but "**Cock-a-doodle-doo!**" was all
the rooster said, of course!

The largest pup was Thomas, who
was calm and so polite,
and next came naughty Horace,
clearly looking for a fight.

Tall Bridget was the third, and then
came Paula, Steve and Fred;
the seventh one was Edward,
but they also called him Ed.

The eighth and final puppy born was really very small,
and needed such a name to make her seem so big and tall.
Her parents named her Bella, just like Spain's first queen…
but as to what she's called—now that's a different thing.

Soon Bella faded back into a very different name—
when "Pipsqueak" was what stuck, the pup did not complain.

Our Pipsqueak always felt left out, so
    different and alone;
she sat and watched her siblings play
    and wished that she had grown.
Their favorite game was keep away, a
    perfect four-on-four…
but Horace snapped at Pip, "You'll just
    mess up the score."

So Pipsqueak sat and watched the
    game, tears stinging her eyes;
she scratched the dirt and rubbed her
    nose while trying not to cry.

But soon she felt an acorn as it whizzed right past her ear— another hit her foot, and then a third one smacked her rear!

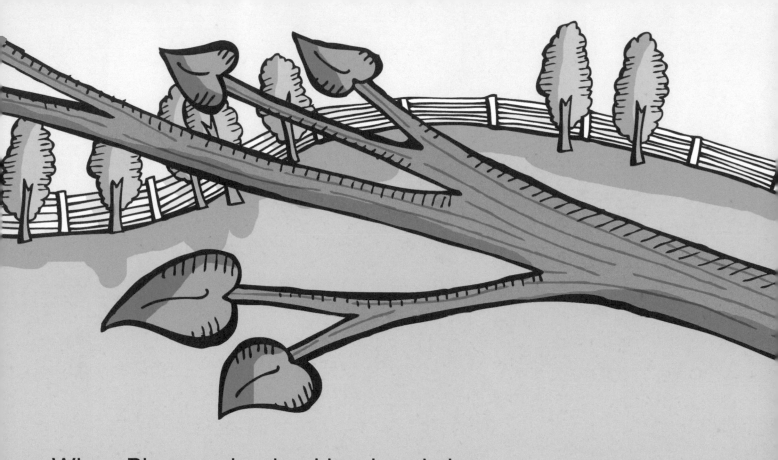

When Pipsqueak raised her head she
was annoyed by what she saw.
"You mind?" she asked a squirrel
munching acorns in his jaw.
The squirrel flopped back softly
on the branch above her head,
and looked with some amusement
at the pup beneath his bed.

"You go and play your silly
    game," he called to her with glee.
"You pups don't seem to know how
    calm and lovely life can be."
Well talking to a chubby squirrel—
    puppies just don't do…
but Pipsqueak always sat alone and
    hadn't any clue.

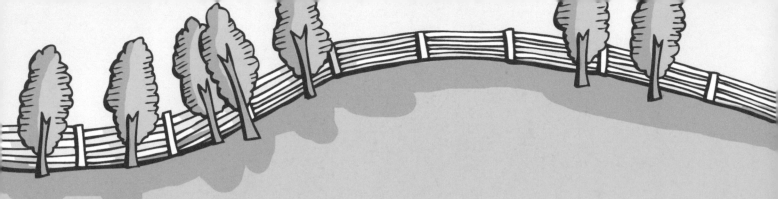

"And what's your name?" She asked the squirrel,
her eyes were open wide.
"It's Chuck," he answered simply.
"You want to come inside?"
He scurried down the tree,
pulled back a curtain
made of bark—
inside the trunk he'd
made a home: so
quiet, sweet and dark.
"Now why would you
ask me inside?"
said Pipsqueak
to the squirrel.
"You know a dog of
any kind could eat
you in one swirl."

"I think you won't," he said simply, and
that was when she knew:
he's very old and pretty plump, his
instinct must come through.
"I've been around a long, long
time," said Chuck to his
new friend.
"I didn't get this old and plump
in only one weekend.
I'm smart enough to get away
when danger comes
my way—
and it sure seems to me
that you could use a
friend today."

Since Pipsqueak thought about it and it made a lot of sense,
she shuffled her paws and settled down, only a little tense.
"I don't know why you play that game," announced her new
    friend Chuck.
"It looks so dull, with just a ball and dogs running amok."

"I like to play," she softly said. "I simply
    don't know how.
My brother says that having me is worse
    than when without."
"But you can play," said sweet old Chuck.
    "Take this advice from me.
When you are small, you must play smart—
    that's what sets you free."

HOME SWEET HO

"Since dogs like you are fast and big with
noses sharp and strong,
a little squirrel needs to have some
smarts to get along.
See I've survived for all these years,
and not from strength or might—
but I've escaped from danger by
avoiding any fight."

So Pipsqueak paused a
   minute and she thought
   for just a spell—
and then she knew just
   how to play the game
   and do it well!
"The game is won when
   someone takes the ball
   and gets away.
I'm small for sure, but
   clever too!" and she got
   up to play!

When Pipsqueak looked at Chuck, in
    just that moment, he was scared…
and when her tongue clobbered his face—
    sweet Chuck was not prepared!
He fell and laughed then got up slowly back
    onto his feet.
She ran away over the field and heard:
    "Let's go Pipsqueak!"

When Pipsqueak shouted
"Horace!" she was
feeling super bold.
"You let me play!" She
barked at him, and felt
her plan unfold.
Well Horace rolled his
eyes at Pipsqueak's
itty-bitty bark.
"No thanks," he barked
back at her, his intent
was mean and stark.
"It's fine," lolled big
old Thomas, always
easy, free and fun.
"Be on our team,
it's no big deal,
the game is
nearly won."

The best spot for our
little Pip was just left
of the ball,
and to the right was
Bridget (who was
really very tall).
The whistle blew and
Pip knew it was time
to make her move:
she pushed the ball
right under Bridget,
getting in her groove!

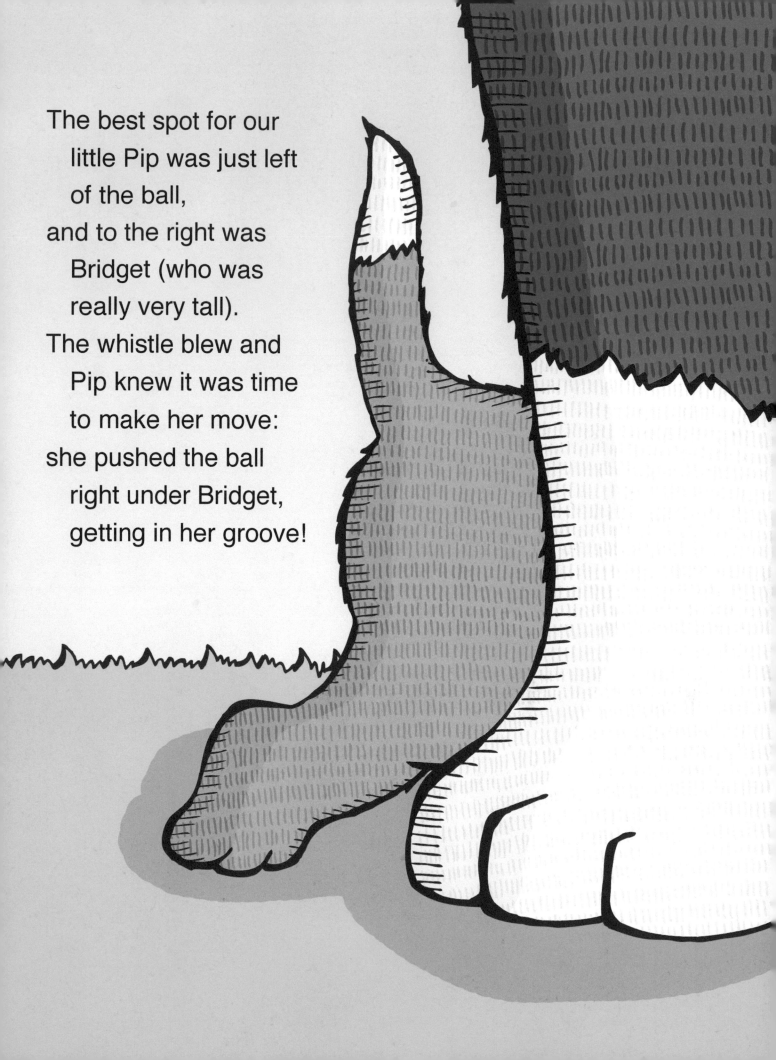

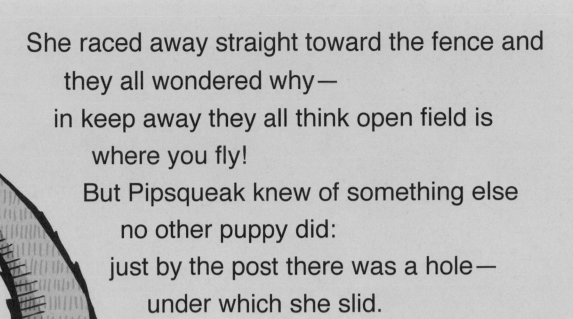

She raced away straight toward the fence and
they all wondered why—
in keep away they all think open field is
where you fly!
But Pipsqueak knew of something else
no other puppy did:
just by the post there was a hole—
under which she slid.

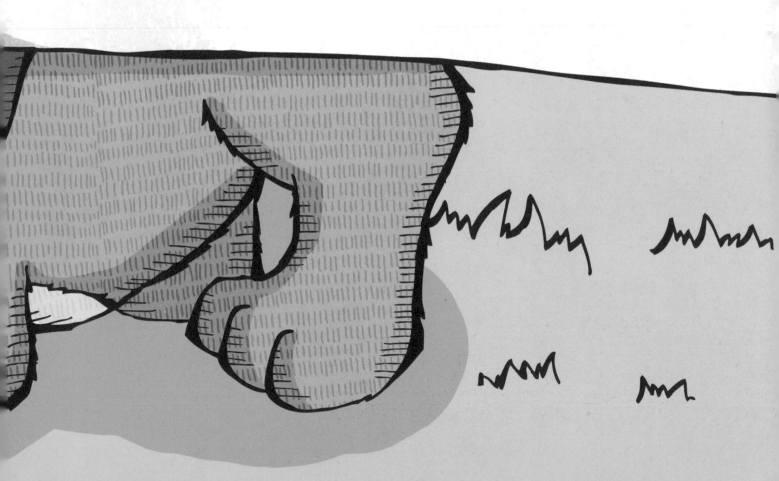

When Horace roared into the fence,
    our Pip was right outside;
and Thomas rolled with laughter at
    his brother's wounded pride.
As Bridget stood completely still,
    not sure of what went down,
the happy puppies all agreed that
    Pip won that day's crown!

Then Horace struggled to his feet and groaned congratulations;
"How did you think to go in there?" he asked with admiration.
"Well keep away is tough for me," our little Pipsqueak said,
"I needed a new strategy, like to escape instead."

"I learned from a new friend that I cannot be someone else—
I had to find a way to use my strengths and be myself.
And being fast and big was not the only way to win;
I had to play in my own way," she answered with a grin.

So Pipsqueak always got to play, on every
    day that followed;
and Horace finally acquiesced, his grudge
    he simply swallowed.
Most days she found a way to make her
    size give her some luck,
and when she wanted her best friend, she
    went to visit Chuck.

THE END

MEET THE AUTHOR AND iLLUSTRATOR

LiSSA WEBBER is constantly inspired by her children and her writing is no exception. Their love of reading and the natural world compelled her to write a story about someone with whom they could identify: a lovable puppy who is too small to do the things she wants to. She is delighted to be donating 100% of the proceeds from this book to Children's Healthcare of Atlanta, where her son received a life-saving surgery when he was under a year old. Lissa lives in Atlanta and loves painting, cooking, and spending time with her wonderful husband, their exceptional children, and sweet puppy Ladybug.

TAMi BOYCE is a Charleston-based illustrator and graphic designer with a fun and whimsical style.

"Holding a pencil in my hand has been my passion for as long as I can remember. I count myself as an extremely lucky individual because I have been able to make a career out of it. We all live in a very serious world, and I like to use my quirky style to remind us of the love, joy, and humor that is often overlooked around us."

To see more of Tami's work, visit tamiboyce.com.

CPSIA information can be obtained
at www.ICGtesting.com
Printed in the USA
LVHW071243271018
595048LV00026BA/836/P